HEAVYWEIGHT
TAKEDOWN

BY JAKE MADDOX

text by
Blake Hoena

STONE ARCH BOOKS
a capstone imprint

Jake Maddox JV books are published by Stone Arch Books
A Capstone Imprint
1710 Roe Crest Drive
North Mankato, Minnesota 56003
www.capstonepub.com

Library of Congress Cataloging-in-Publication Data

Maddox, Jake, author.
 Heavyweight takedown / by Jake Maddox ; text by Blake Hoena.
    pages cm. -- (Jake Maddox JV)
 Summary: Ninth-grader Kyle has always been the heavyweight on his junior high school wrestling team, but when a new kid shows up he loses the challenge and finds himself relegated to the B-team — until a girl on the squad suggests he move down a weight class.
 ISBN 978-1-4342-9638-2 (library binding) -- ISBN 978-1-4342-9670-2 (pbk.) -- ISBN 978-1-4965-0179-0 (ebook PDF)
1. Wrestling--Juvenile fiction. 2. Competition (Psychology)--Juvenile fiction. 3. Self-confidence--Juvenile fiction. 4. Friendship--Juvenile fiction. 5. Junior high schools--Juvenile fiction. [1. Wrestling--Fiction. 2. Competition (Psychology)--Fiction. 3. Self-confidence--Fiction. 4. Friendship--Fiction. 5. Junior high schools--Fiction. 6. Schools--Fiction.] I. Hoena, B. A., author. II. Title.

 PZ7.M25643He 2015
 813.6--dc23

2014023847

This book has been officially leveled by using the F&P Text Level Gradient™ Leveling System.

Art Director: Heather Kindseth
Designer: Veronica Scott
Production Specialist: Jennifer Walker

Photo Credits:
Shutterstock: Chamnong Inthasaro, cover (background), chapter openings, Nicholas Piccillo, cover, back cover
Design Elements: Shutterstock

Printed in China by Nordica.
0914/CA21401508
092014   008470NORDS15

TABLE OF CONTENTS

CHAPTER 1

THE TANK

As ninth grader Kyle McGregor strutted through the halls of Benjamin Franklin Junior High School, everyone moved out of his way. And with good reason. At 5'8" and nearly 180 pounds, he was bigger than most of the other kids.

Kyle had always been big for his age, and in sports it helped him out. His teammates called him "Tank" because he could bowl over any opponent on the wrestling mat or on the football field.

Kyle was a standout offensive lineman on the Jets' football team, and no defender could push him around. But now, with the leaves changing colors outside, it was time for Kyle to turn his attention to his favorite sport — wrestling.

Wrestling at Ben Franklin Junior High was a no-cut sport. Everyone who wanted to wrestle got to be part of the team. Next year in high school, however, that wouldn't be the case.

One more year before I can try out for a spot on the varsity team, Kyle thought as he strolled down the hallway. *One more year to dominate the junior high heavyweights.*

"What's up, Tank?" one of his football teammates asked as Kyle walked by.

"Not much," Kyle replied with a high five. He didn't have much time to waste. The bell had just rung to mark the end of the school day, and today was the informational meeting to kick off the wrestling season.

At the meeting, the team would get a rundown on the season, go over practice schedules, big matches, tournaments, and new rules in the conference. But Kyle couldn't wait for next week, when the team's real practices would begin.

The truth was, he played football simply because Coach Johnson, who was also his English teacher, had asked him to. He'd been the biggest kid in school since seventh grade, and his size helped him succeed on the gridiron.

But Kyle had joined the wrestling team because he'd *wanted* to. His size was definitely a factor on the mat as well. He dominated nearly every challenger he faced as the Jets' heavyweight.

Being an offensive lineman wasn't much different from being a wrestler. Both positions were all about stance, footwork, keeping your center of gravity low, and fighting for position.

Kyle never felt like he influenced the outcome of the game on the football field, though.

But when he wrestled, whether he won or lost a match, Kyle always had a direct impact on his team's score. He affected the outcome of every meet, and that made him feel important.

Kyle stopped in front of his locker, spun the combination on his lock, and then popped it open to toss his backpack inside before heading to the wrestling room.

Out of the corner of his eye, Kyle saw his best friend Spider coming toward him. Spider's real name was Anthony Eckert, and while he was the same height as Kyle — 5'8" — he weighed about sixty pounds less. When he wasn't wrestling, Spider looked like a jumble of limbs bending awkwardly at pointy knees and elbows. But watching him on the mat, he was amazing. Those long, dangly limbs helped him tangle up his opponents like flies caught in a spiderweb. That's how he had earned his nickname.

"Hey. What's up, Tank?" Spider said, stopping at Kyle's locker.

"Not much," Kyle replied.

"Ready for wrestling season?" Spider asked with a big grin.

Kyle nodded. "Yeah," he said. "I'm pumped to hit the mats next week."

"I'm gonna try for 126 this year," Spider said.

Kyle smiled at that and shook his head. Spider was always trying to move up a weight class or two. He thought the wrestlers in the heavier weight classes got more respect than lightweights. "The bigger, the badder," Spider always said.

Kyle always argued that he didn't understand what that meant, to which Spider replied, "That's because you're already big and bad."

Kyle pushed his locker shut. "You ready?" he asked Spider.

"Yeah, let's go check out the new meat," Spider said, referring to the new seventh graders who'd be joining the team. The older kids were always anxious to see whether there would be anyone good enough to challenge them for their spot.

Kyle and Spider strolled down the hall. A few other wrestlers were headed the same way. They all had similar postures — legs springy, biceps flexed, and backs straight.

His teammates all filed into the gym, but Kyle stayed back. Outside the gym's double doors stood a wall of trophy cases — one for each sport. Kyle peered into the wrestling case.

On the shelves sat row after row of trophies from past tournaments. Most had been won by the Spangle brothers — three local wrestling legends.

The youngest of the Spangle brothers had graduated high school the year before, so Kyle didn't know any of them personally. But he still looked up to them. Like Kyle, the Spangle boys had all wrestled as heavyweights, and they had all dominated on the mats.

A few of the older, dustier trophies had actually been won by the Spangles' father way back when he'd attended school here. Now Mr. Spangle coached the varsity team at Ben Franklin High School. Everyone on the junior high team hoped to eventually wrestle for him on the high school varsity squad.

Because the junior high wrestling season was a few weeks shorter than the high school season, Coach Spangle would sometimes invite the most talented ninth-grade wrestlers on the junior high team to practice with his varsity team for the final few weeks of the season.

If I do a good enough job this season, Kyle thought, *maybe Coach Spangle will invite me to practice with the varsity team.*

Kyle stood there gazing at all of the wrestling trophies, lost in thought, until Spider stuck his head out of the gym doorway.

"Come on, Tank!" Spider called.

Kyle took one last glance at the display case before heading toward the gym. *This is going to be my year,* he thought.

CHAPTER 2

PREP TIME

Inside the wrestling room the air was stuffy, smelling heavily of sweat and disinfectant. The mats were rolled up and pushed against the walls. Kyle and Spider found seats toward the back of the room as the rest of their teammates streamed through the doors.

Even if he didn't recognize many of them, Kyle was sure he could guess what grade each wrestler was in just by glancing at them. The other ninth graders strutted into the room cool and confident, high-fiving each other. Most knew they were top in their weight class and that they would be on A squad — the guys who got to wrestle at all the tournaments.

The eighth graders tried to act calm, but they were looking around nervously. Their eyes darted from the ninth graders, who they would need to challenge to be on A squad, to the seventh graders, who might challenge them for their B-squad spots. The wrestlers on B squad subbed in at meets if one of the guys on A squad couldn't wrestle for some reason.

Kyle spotted some seventh graders, too. They all looked mousy and scared. Most of them would end up on C squad, which meant they would probably only wrestle at all-ages meets, tournaments anyone could enter.

Spider nudged Kyle's arm. "Who's that?" he asked, nodding toward a girl, probably a new seventh grader, who had just walked in.

"Dunno," Kyle said.

"I can't believe Coach would let a girl join the team," Spider said.

"If she can wrestle, why not?" Kyle asked. *Spider's probably worried he'll have to wrestle her,* he thought. *He has enough trouble just talking to girls. Imagine if he had to wrestle one.*

Another new kid walked in right behind the girl and caught Kyle's attention. The new kid was big. He had a few inches on Kyle and shoulders as wide as a bus. *He looks familiar,* Kyle thought.

"There's no way he's in seventh grade," Spider said, also noticing the boy.

"Yeah, I doubt it," Kyle said. "And I swear I've seen him somewhere before."

Finally, Coach Branberg came in. "Okay, boys," he began, holding up a stack of papers. Suddenly noticing the one girl, he added, "I mean, um . . . team. Here are your sign-up sheets to take home for your parents to fill out. Make sure they include their email addresses so I can send practice and tournament schedules. And let them know that we can always use chaperones for away meets."

Coach went on to take attendance. "We'll do our first weigh-in Friday when equipment is handed out. For today, when I call out your name, give me your expected weight class," he said, reading the first name off his clipboard. "Kyle McGregor!"

"Heavyweight!" Kyle announced. He knew he'd make weight. The Jets' conference used standard high school weight classes, with one exception. For high school, heavyweight was 210 and up. But for junior high school, it was anything over 175.

"Anthony Eckert!" Coach called.

"126," Spider answered.

Coach Branberg raised a questioning eyebrow. "You wrestled at 120 last year. You sure about that? We probably have Trevor at 126, too." Coach looked toward Trevor Knox, another ninth grader, who nodded in agreement.

"Yeah, Coach," Spider replied with a smile. "I had a growth spurt."

That got a chuckle from his teammates. Spider was constantly trying to pack on pounds and wrestle at a higher weight class. If Coach let him, he would probably choose to wrestle as a heavyweight.

Last season, Spider had downed a milk shake with every meal to try to gain weight, but all the sugar had only made him hyper. He'd ended up burning off all the extra calories he got from the shakes because he couldn't stop talking and running around. The season before that, Spider had tried eating steak for every meal, but his dad had quickly complained about the cost. This season, Kyle knew, his friend was sure to try some other scheme.

"Avery Spangle!" Coach called. "Ah, Coach Spangle's kid?"

"120," the girl answered. "And yes."

"Did you hear that?" Spider whispered. "I didn't know the Spangle brothers had a sister! Do you really think Coach will let her wrestle at 120? She can't weigh much more than a hundred pounds."

"Dunno," Kyle said. "But who else is going to wrestle at that weight? Joel?"

Spider scrunched up his nose. Joel Flesher was an eighth grader who weighed in at 120. Last year, Spider had always beat him at practice. "My little sister could beat Joel," Spider said with a snort.

Just then Coach motioned to the huge kid sitting next to Avery. "For those of you who don't know, this is Kenny Tasker. He's in eighth grade," Coach announced. "He just transferred here from St. Irene's, since they were forced to cancel their wrestling program this year."

St. Irene's was a small private school nearby. Usually their team only had a dozen or so wrestlers. Last season, St. Irene's had hosted a citywide invitational, hoping to boost interest in its wrestling program. Kyle and Spider had both attended the meet. But if Kenny had transferred to Ben Franklin Junior High, obviously that meet hadn't saved St. Irene's wrestling program.

"That's where I recognize him from," Kyle whispered to Spider. "I knew he looked familiar."

"Yeah, I remember him," Spider said. "He was by far their best wrestler."

The St. Irene's invitational had been broken down into age groups to allow more kids to wrestle. Kyle had won his age group and weight class, and if he recalled correctly, so had Kenny.

Then Coach asked Kenny, "Weight class?"

"Heavyweight," Kenny replied.

Spider nudged Kyle. "Looks like you aren't the only heavyweight on the team anymore," he said.

Kenny looks lean, but he must be made of muscle, Kyle thought. Still, he wasn't worried that Kenny would take his spot on A squad. Not yet.

CHAPTER 3

WEIGH-INS

For the rest of that week, Spider couldn't stop talking about Avery. Kyle wasn't sure if it was because his friend was afraid he'd have to wrestle her or if it was because he had a crush on her.

"I can't believe we have a girl on the team," Spider kept saying. "I don't want to wrestle a girl. Have you ever wrestled one? Do you think she's as good as her brothers?"

Kyle just rolled his eyes. Spider was probably as nervous about having to touch a girl as he was about the possibility of losing a match to one.

When Friday finally came around, equipment was handed out, and the team had their first weigh-in. Everyone was fitted for a maroon-colored team singlet. Then Coach handed out ear guards, kneepads, and mouthguards.

Once everyone had their gear, Coach had the team line up for weigh-ins. Spider started it off, weighing in at 122.

"Aw, come on. I weighed 123 last night," he said, frustrated.

"Next time, don't hit the bathroom before weigh-ins!" someone yelled, and the rest of the team chuckled.

Coach remained serious, though. "Either way," he said to Spider, "it's a little light for 126." Then to the rest of team he yelled, "Keep it moving!"

As Kyle watched his friend get off the scale, he saw Spider gulp anxiously and glance at Avery. Kyle knew Spider was probably nervous that Coach Branberg would ask him to drop a couple pounds so he could wrestle at 120. That would mean he'd be in the same weight class as Avery.

When Kyle stepped onto the scale, he weighed in at 179, which easily made him a heavyweight.

Now all I have to do is maintain my weight, Kyle thought as he went to sit down at the back of the room to watch the other wrestlers weigh in.

Next up was Avery, who weighed in at 108 pounds. Everyone was shocked that she weighed as much as that. But seeing her in her singlet, it was clear that she was ripped. When she stretched out her arms, the cut of her triceps was visible.

"That puts you at 113, Avery," Coach said. "What do you think? You still want to try for 120?"

"Yeah, Coach," Avery replied.

Hearing that, Spider turned to Kyle. "If Coach doesn't let me wrestle at 126, he shouldn't let her wrestle at 120," he mumbled.

Next it was Kenny's turn. He topped the scales at 186. Kyle knew Kenny was big, but he didn't think he would weigh in that heavy. Kyle was starting to feel a little worried. He'd just lost the title of biggest kid at school.

He looked his fellow heavyweight up and down, and for the first time in his life, Kyle McGregor felt small.

* * *

Practice started the following Monday. Early in the season, Coach liked to focus on strength and endurance, so that first day, the team hit the weight room hard. Kyle hated this part of practice. He was sweating through his T-shirt, and all the lifting and repetitions were wearing him out.

After their session in the weight room, Coach separated the wrestlers by squad and had them do stick wrestling, an exercise that required two wrestlers to hold onto the same wooden rod. The goal was to try to gain control of the stick while keeping a good wrestling stance. Since Kyle was the biggest wrestler on A squad, nobody could drag him around. He just held on to the stick and let the other wrestlers do all the work.

Between his bouts, Kyle watched Kenny. The new kid seemed to be winning the stick wrestling easily as well. He was tossing everyone on B squad around like they were puppets.

So far, Kyle's only exchange with Kenny had been a "hey" as they passed by one another in the hall. Kenny seemed shy. He hadn't talked to any of the wrestlers much either . . . except for Avery.

I wonder how they know each other, Kyle thought.

"Nervous?" Spider asked when he caught Kyle watching Kenny.

"Nah," Kyle replied, even though he kind of was. He nodded in Avery's direction. "You?"

"No way," Spider said. "I'm wrestling at 126. She's at 120."

"Yeah, sure," Kyle replied. "We'll see what Coach says about that."

Spider just huffed in response.

After practice, Coach called a team meeting. "Next week, we wrestle Jefferson," he began. "As the returning wrestlers know, I want to be sure the best athletes are representing the team — particularly for A squad." Coach paced at the front of the room. "So starting a week from today," he said, "we'll have wrestle-offs every Monday for the rest of the season. Anyone on B or C squad can challenge anyone on the next squad for their spot. So C squad, you can challenge B squad, and B squad, you can challenge A squad. Got it?"

Kyle looked around the room. Everyone was eyeing the other wrestlers in their weight class. Spider was checking out Trevor, whom he would have to challenge for the 126 A-squad spot. Avery was staring down Joel, the other wrestler at 120. And Kyle saw Kenny sneaking glances at him.

"For now, returning wrestlers will initially be given their spots on A squad or B squad because they were on the team last season. But starting next Monday, anyone can make one challenge per week," Coach said. "Returning wrestlers — you will have to earn your spots. If you're on A squad and you win against a B-squad wrestler, you will keep your spot. If the B-squad wrestler wins, he or she might get to move up to A squad. But I'll make all final decisions about who represents each squad at our meets. Does that make sense?"

Everyone nodded, so Coach yelled, "See you tomorrow!" With that, the wrestlers began to file out toward the locker room.

As Kyle stood up to walk out of the room, he bumped into Kenny. "What's up?" Kyle asked him.

"Hey," Kenny said, quickly turning away from Kyle and heading for the doors.

Spider was leaning against the wall just outside the wrestling room, waiting for Kyle. "Hey, I heard Kenny's going to try for A squad," he whispered as he watched Kenny walk out of the gym with Avery.

"How do you know?" Kyle asked. "We just left."

"I just heard him talking to Avery," Spider said.

"Oh," Kyle replied, trying to act calm. But he got a nervous feeling in his stomach.

Kenny will have to challenge me before he can wrestle on the A squad, he thought as he walked toward his locker. *What if he beats me and I'm no longer the team's heavyweight?*

* * *

As the week went on and Kyle saw how skilled a wrestler Kenny was, he got more and more nervous. Kyle knew he'd have to learn some new moves if he wanted a chance at beating Kenny. So each night after practice, dinner, and homework, Kyle sat at the computer and studied videos of different wrestling moves.

That weekend, Kyle came across the guillotine, a move Coach had let them try a few times at practice. If Kyle could get it down, the guillotine would be tough to beat. The goal of the move was to get an opponent to move to his back. But in order to master it, Kyle would need someone to practice on.

Luckily, Kyle's dad was always willing to be his practice dummy. But this time, when Kyle explained the move, his dad sounded hesitant.

"You want to do what?" Dad asked.

"Just get on your hands and knees," Kyle explained, "in a defensive starting position."

Kyle wrapped his right leg around his dad's for a leg hook. Then he pulled his dad's left arm back and forced his head underneath it, turning his dad's arm and head around and rolling him onto his back. Each time he was about to secure the final hold, however, Kyle lost his leg hook, and his dad escaped. After he escaped for the third time in as many tries, Kyle sighed in frustration.

"Let's call it quits for today, bud," Dad said. "You'll get it eventually."

Eventually isn't quick enough, Kyle thought.

CHAPTER 4

WRESTLE-OFF

On Monday, Kyle felt more nervous than he could ever remember being about a match. He wasn't used to wrestling stronger or bigger opponents, and he didn't feel ready to face Kenny.

After the last class of the day, Spider met Kyle by his locker.

"You ready for this?" Spider asked as they walked toward the wrestling room.

"You bet," Kyle lied.

Kyle had never been challenged for his spot on A squad before. Until Kenny had showed up, he had been the only heavyweight at school. Even at meets, he'd never had much competition. There weren't many kids his age and size. Oftentimes, the teams the Jets faced didn't even have an actual heavyweight. Sometimes those teams would choose to have a wrestler at the 175 weight class go up against Kyle just so they wouldn't have to forfeit the heavyweight match. And Kyle almost always won his matches against smaller opponents.

As Kyle warmed up, he realized that Kenny provided him a real challenge for a change. But that didn't help calm Kyle's nerves.

After warm-ups, the team got ready to watch the day's wrestle-offs. Kyle sat in the back of the wrestling room where he could keep an eye on the challenges and continue to do warm-up exercises at the same time.

There weren't many challenges that day. The seventh graders were too afraid to take on the older wrestlers . . . all except for Avery, at least.

Avery challenged Joel for the B-squad 120-weight spot. Joel had a few inches on Avery and more than ten pounds, which should have helped him. Unfortunately for him, he didn't get into a good stance at the start of the match, and that cost him.

Standing almost straight up, Joel staggered forward as if he was going to pick Avery up in a bear hug. When he went to reach for her, Avery grabbed his arm and yanked him forward for an arm drag. Then she went in for a single-leg takedown. Joel never fully recovered after that, and he ended up losing the match by a few points.

Coach must have been impressed. He walked up to the whiteboard at the front of the room to adjust the rankings. He erased Avery's name from the C-squad 120 weight class, and wrote Joel's name there in its place. Then he erased Joel's name from the B-squad spot and put Avery's name in that spot.

The A-squad 120 weight class slot was still open, though, and Avery noticed.

"Who's going to take the A-squad spot?" she asked, her face turning red.

"That's to be determined," Coach replied. "You only challenged for B squad in this wrestle-off."

Avery stomped off the mat with a huff and sat down, leaning against the wall at the back of the room. She looked angry.

After a couple of other wrestle-offs, Spider challenged Trevor for the A-squad spot at 126.

"Okay, Spider, here's the deal," Coach said before the match began. "I'll let you wrestle for the 126 spot now, but if you lose, I want you at 120 on A squad. Agreed?"

"Okay," Spider said, sounding defeated.

Kyle shook his head at his friend's obvious disappointment. *After his weigh-in, Spider should have known this was coming*, Kyle thought. *120 is just a more natural weight for him.*

Spider did end up losing the wrestle-off for the A-squad spot at 126, but only by a point. Spider was still clearly the better wrestler, but Trevor had a size advantage. He was bigger and stronger and spent most of the match pushing Spider around.

As Coach adjusted the rankings, putting Spider in the 120 A-squad spot, Avery looked really upset, and Kyle saw her walk quietly out of the room.

Kyle could understand her being upset. But the truth was, while Avery was a good wrestler, Spider was bigger than her, and he had more experience.

Maybe she'll move to 113 now, Kyle thought.

"Any more challenges?" Coach asked, turning back to the team.

Kenny stood up and nodded toward Kyle. "I'm trying for heavyweight, A squad," Kenny said.

Kyle gulped nervously. As he looked around the room, his fellow A-squad wrestlers avoided meeting his gaze. They knew this was a serious challenge. Kenny wasn't some inexperienced new wrestler. As Spider had said, he'd been St. Irene's best wrestler last season.

Kyle could feel the tension in the room as he and Kenny walked to the mat. After they bumped fists, Coach blew his whistle to start the match.

Kyle decided to go on offense right away. He rushed in, hoping to grapple with his taller opponent. Usually if he got in close, Kyle had the advantage because of his low center of gravity. Most of his opponents just couldn't budge him, so once he got his opponent off balance, he'd move in for a takedown.

But Kenny surprised him with the same move that Avery had used earlier on Joel. He grabbed Kyle's arm for an arm drag. When Kyle stumbled forward, Kenny grabbed his lead leg for a single-leg takedown.

One second, Kenny was lifting Kyle's leg into the air . . . the next, Kyle was on his back. And that meant two points went to Kenny for the takedown.

Kyle quickly spun onto his stomach. Kenny went for a half nelson, trying to wrap an arm around Kyle's arms and neck to twist him over onto his back again. Kenny was strong, but Kyle managed to fight out of it and escape for one point.

By the time he was back on his feet, Kyle was breathing heavily, but it looked like Kenny hadn't even broken a sweat. Kyle couldn't remember ever wrestling against someone as athletic or as strong as Kenny.

Kyle didn't do much better the rest of the match. He kept things close, but he couldn't catch his breath or get Kenny out of position. And he certainly didn't have a good enough handle on the guillotine to use it on Kenny just yet.

When Coach adjusted the rankings after the match, Kenny was on A squad and, for the first time ever, Kyle had been moved down to B squad.

CHAPTER 5

B SQUAD

At the meet against Jefferson on Friday, Kyle sat on the bench watching his teammates compete. *I've never felt so useless on this team before,* he thought. *For the first time since seventh grade, I'll have no impact on the outcome of the meet.*

"That should be me out there," Avery said, interrupting Kyle's thoughts.

Kyle looked over at her, but her eyes were glued to the match. It was the A-squad 120-weight match, and the wrestler from Jefferson was putting up a good fight against Spider.

Kyle and Avery had never exchanged more than a quick hello before, so it surprised him how openly she spoke her mind just then.

"Come on, you're just in seventh grade," Kyle said.

"So? My brothers all made the A squad in seventh grade," she said. "I bet you did, too."

"Yeah, but not right away," Kyle replied.

Kyle was amazed at Avery's confidence. But he could understand where it came from. After all, she had grown up in a wrestling family. And not just any wrestling family — the famed Spangle wrestling family.

Avery and Kyle kept watching Spider's match. With his opponent's arms wrapped around his head, Spider slipped out of a headlock and then sprang to his feet for an escape, scoring a point.

"I kind of know how you feel," Kyle said, glancing over to where Kenny was warming up for his match.

"You shouldn't feel bad losing to him," Avery said. "Kenny's my cousin. He's wrestled with my brothers for years. He's just as good as they were, if not better."

"No way! Seriously? I wondered how you two knew each other. He hardly talks to anyone else," Kyle said.

"Well, he hasn't exactly felt welcome on the team. Spider's been a jerk to both of us because he doesn't want me wrestling," she said. "Plus, I think Kenny's missing his friends at his old school."

"That's understandable," Kyle said. "I hope I'm not coming off as a jerk, too."

She shook her head and smiled. "Not yet."

Trying not to sound jealous, Kyle asked, "So, did your brothers teach you some moves, too?"

"Really? You, too?" Avery said. She gave him a knowing smile. "It's funny how everyone looks up to my brothers because of some trophies they won years ago. But imagine what it was like having

them practice their moves on you all the time —
whether you wanted them to or not."

"Must have been rough," Kyle said.

"Luckily, my mom's a tough ref," Avery joked.

They turned back to Spider's match. He'd just
surprised his opponent, scooping up his ankle and
pulling his leg out from under him for an ankle
pick. His opponent fell to the mat, and Spider
scored two points for a takedown. That put him
up 12–4. He was on his way to scoring a major
decision, a win of eight or more points.

"This was supposed to be my year," Kyle said,
glancing over at Kenny again. "I was sure I'd win
most of my matches on A squad."

Avery looked Kyle up and down. "Why don't
you drop down a weight class?" she asked.

"What, wrestle at 175?" Kyle asked, looking at
her in disbelief.

"Yeah, you've been wrestling heavyweights all
along," she explained, "so you'd have an advantage

against the smaller guys. It'd be easier for you to win at a lower weight. You're actually kind of small for a heavyweight. Plus, you'd have a good shot at getting back on A squad."

"But —" Kyle began.

"It's what my brother Tim did in high school," Avery interrupted. "And he won state two years in a row."

She seems pretty sure of herself, Kyle thought. *Having your dad as a wrestling coach must help.* "I'll think about it," he said.

But Avery wasn't done. "Wrestling's not all about what *you* want, you know. You need to do what's best for the team," she said, nodding in Spider's direction. "We needed someone to wrestle at 120. That's why I challenged at that weight. It wasn't anything against your friend."

Kyle understood that. He wished Spider would see it that way, too, instead of being angry that Avery was challenging for the spot he had last year.

"I'm not sure why he's always trying to move up a weight class," Kyle said.

"Probably just some macho guy thing," Avery said. "The bigger, the badder."

Hearing her repeat Spider's saying made Kyle chuckle. *Spider could learn a thing or two from Avery,* Kyle thought, smiling to himself.

* * *

Spider and Kenny both won major decisions to help the Jets take the meet. Kyle wasn't sure how he should feel. He was happy for his team, but he was also frustrated that he'd played no part in their victory other than rooting them on from the bench.

After the meet, Kyle waited outside the locker room for Spider. He couldn't stop thinking about what Avery had suggested.

She's right, Kyle thought. *Wrestling is a team sport. Everyone's individual scores are added up to determine the winning team. If there's a weakness at one spot, it needs to be filled. That's why Avery challenged Joel for the 120 spot. But if there's a solid wrestler like Kenny at a weight class, and he keeps winning . . . why mess with it?*

Just then, Spider pushed through the locker room door. "Hey," he said.

Without greeting him, Kyle asked the question he couldn't stop thinking about, "Do you think I should drop to 175?"

"What? No way! You're our heavyweight," Spider exclaimed, scrunching up his nose.

"Tonight I wasn't," Kyle replied.

"Don't worry about it," Spider said. "You can challenge Kenny to a wrestle-off on Monday."

"But what if I can't beat him?" Kyle asked.

"You will," Spider said, sounding almost angry at the possibility that Kyle might lose. Then Spider headed toward the doors to the parking lot. "We gotta meet my dad," he said. "He's taking us out for burgers."

Kyle shook his head and raced after his friend.

CHAPTER 6

CUTTING WEIGHT

"So, tell me what happened," Spider's dad said as he tucked into his burger at the restaurant.

Spider broke down his match move by move as he nibbled on his French fries and took sips of his chocolate milk shake.

Kyle zoned out as he thought about cutting weight. *Kenny and I could battle it out for the heavyweight spot, but would that really help the team? We'd just be beating up on each other instead of on our opponents,* he thought as he twirled his straw around in his shake.

If I want to get back on A squad, cutting weight is the obvious way to do that, Kyle decided. *Liam just lost his match, and I've been practicing really hard. That weight class is clearly a weak spot in our lineup.*

"So, Dad, Kyle is thinking of dropping down to 175," Spider said, interrupting Kyle's thoughts.

"Really? Is it because of that new wrestler Anthony mentioned?" Spider's dad asked, pausing in between bites of his burger.

"Yeah. Kenny Tasker," Kyle said. "He's good. Better than good. He's Spangle good."

"Huh?" Spider looked stunned. He put his hamburger down on his plate.

"I was talking to Avery during your match —" Kyle explained.

"Why were you talking to her?" Spider snapped, but Kyle continued his explanation.

"She said they're cousins. Kenny has wrestled with the Spangle brothers for years now. He knows their moves. Plus, he's way bigger than me," Kyle explained.

"So? You've beaten wrestlers taller than you before," Spider said.

"Kenny's not just taller. He has almost ten pounds on me," Kyle said. "And it's ten pounds of muscle. He's really strong and fast."

"So?" Spider said again.

Kyle just shook his head. Clearly his friend didn't want to hear it.

Spider's dad tried to keep the conversation going, but Spider and Kyle didn't talk much after that. They just ate their burgers and drank their shakes. Actually, Kyle didn't even finish his. If he was going to cut weight, that meant cutting out junk food, too.

* * *

Over the weekend, Kyle made a plan. The first thing he did was check out the Jets' wrestling website. He went to the student section, where

Coach had created a whole page of healthy food suggestions such as fresh juice instead of soda and veggies instead of chips. His motto was, "Keep it lean, and eat what your body needs." Coach had even created a balanced meal plan for the wrestlers to follow if they wanted to.

That afternoon, Kyle ran into his mom in the kitchen as he went to wash off an apple for a snack. "Could we have broiled fish and salad for dinner tonight?" he asked her.

"Really?" Kyle's mom said. She seemed surprised. "You mean I can make something that's not fried?"

Kyle had never worried about cutting weight before. Up until now, his team had always needed a heavyweight, so he'd simply maintained his weight. While many of his teammates had been eating healthy foods and putting in extra time at the gym, Kyle had been eating pizza and playing video games.

"Yeah, I'm thinking of cutting a little weight," he told his mom.

"I think losing a few pounds could be healthy, as long as you're smart about it," his mother said. "How about I help you come up with a list of healthy snacks and meals you can eat, and then we can go to the grocery store to pick up some items?"

"That sounds awesome," Kyle said, smiling.

* * *

After school on Monday, Kyle headed toward the seventh-grade lockers to look for Avery. He found her surrounded by a group of girls. "Hey, Avery," he said, interrupting them.

They all turned toward him, surprised a ninth-grade boy was stopping to talk. Then Avery's friends quickly backed away, all smiles and giggles.

"What's up, Tank? Ready for practice?" Avery asked.

"Remember what we were talking about at Friday's meet?" Kyle asked.

"Yeah, about you —" Avery started.

Kyle quickly cut her off. "Let's keep it a secret," he said. "Only you and Spider know."

"Okay," Avery replied.

"I think I'm going to do it. I just want to okay it with Coach at the weigh-in on Friday," Kyle added.

"Good idea," Avery said, nodding.

Once Avery gathered her wrestling things, the two of them headed toward the gym together. As Avery walked off toward the girls' locker room, Kyle ran into Spider.

"What was that about?" Spider asked, sounding suspicious.

"Just talking wrestling," Kyle said. "Sheesh, what's up with you?"

"I've been talking to Brandon and Ryan," Spider said. "And none of us want to wrestle Avery."

"Why?" Kyle asked. "Are you afraid you'll lose to her?"

"No," Spider said, shaking his head. "Because she's a girl. We don't want to wrestle a girl."

"What does that have to do with anything?" Kyle asked.

"Everything," Spider said, his voice rising to a screech.

Out of the corner of his eye, Kyle noticed that some of the other wrestlers were starting to stare in their direction. Kyle just didn't understand why Spider's nervousness around girls was turning into anger. But before Kyle could respond, Coach walked into the gym.

"A squad with me!" he yelled, moving into the wrestling room.

CHAPTER 7

TEAM TENSION

That week of practice was long and tough. Kyle sensed some distance from Spider. He wasn't sure if it was simply because they weren't on the A squad together anymore or if it was really because Kyle was becoming friends with Avery.

Whatever it was, Kyle was trying not to let it bother him. He was on a mission. With his mom's help, he was eating healthier than he ever had before. He was doing push-ups and sit-ups during downtime at practice. He was even fitting in some extra sprints on the outdoor track after practice each day while he waited for his dad to come pick him up.

Friday morning, Kyle decided to swing by Avery's locker. He wanted to tell her that he'd weighed himself on his parents' scale that morning, and his weight had been an even 177.

But I'll do an official weigh-in at practice today, Kyle thought. *And that's when I'll talk to Coach about dropping to 175.*

As Kyle walked down the hallway, he saw Brandon, Ryan, and Spider standing by Avery's locker. *That's weird,* Kyle thought as he walked toward the group.

The boys' backs were to Kyle, but Avery was facing him, and she looked upset. Kyle could hear the boys taunting her as he got closer to them.

"We just don't want you on the team anymore," Brandon said.

"Girls aren't as strong as boys," Ryan said. "Or as good at wrestling."

"Yeah, and — and —" Spider stammered.

Kyle walked up to the group. "What's up, guys?" he said, acting like nothing was wrong.

The boys all stopped talking and glared at him.

"We're just having a talk with Avery about what's best for the wrestling team," Ryan said.

"Yeah? And what would that be?" Kyle asked, looking around at the group. No one responded.

Avery looked mad, like she was about to start screaming at all of them, so Kyle pulled his other teammates away. "Seriously, guys," he said to them. "Do you really want to mess with Avery Spangle? Just think what would happen if her brothers found out you were being mean to her."

"Whatever, Tank," Spider said, turning away. Brandon and Ryan both took a last look at Kyle and then followed Spider down the hall.

None of them want to have one, let alone three of the Spangle brothers coming after them, Kyle thought, watching them stalk off down the hall.

Then Kyle turned around to see if Avery was okay. She was busy gathering her books for class.

"Hey, Avery, sorry about th—" Kyle started.

But before Kyle could get his words out, Avery whipped her head around and shouted, "Your friends are jerks! Just leave me alone." And then she stomped off in the opposite direction.

* * *

Practice was tense that afternoon. Avery didn't show up, and Kyle was concerned about his new friend. Spider wasn't talking to Kyle, and Brandon and Ryan kept glaring at him across the wrestling room.

Trying not to let it upset him too much, Kyle decided to put his energy and focus into practice.

Coach Branberg started practice off with a weigh-in. Spider now weighed 120, so he would officially be wrestling at the 120 A-squad spot in tournaments. As expected, Kyle weighed in at 177, which raised some eyebrows — mostly Coach's.

There would be another wrestle-off Monday, but Kyle knew he wouldn't be ready to wrestle at 175 yet. *I need another week at least,* he thought.

During a water break, Kyle hung back as the other wrestlers filed out of the room to visit the water fountain.

"Hey, Coach," Kyle began. "Can I talk to you about something? I've been thinking of cutting weight."

The news didn't seem to surprise Coach Branberg. "I always thought 175 was a more natural weight for you," he said. "But since we didn't have another heavyweight, I wasn't going to ask you to cut weight. Just don't do anything crazy. Make sure you're losing weight in a healthy way."

"I'm following your guidelines on the website and running extra sprints," Kyle replied.

"That's all it takes," Coach said, gently punching Kyle's shoulder. "Good to see you putting in the effort."

CHAPTER 8

DUCK UNDER

On Monday morning, Kyle ran into Avery in the hallway in between classes. "Hey, Avery," Kyle said as he walked toward her. "You weren't at practice on Friday. What's up?"

"Your friends made it pretty clear that I'm not wanted on the team," she said, turning away.

Kyle chased after her. "Hey, they're just afraid they'll get beat by a girl," he said, forcing a laugh.

The response Kyle got was not what he'd expected. Avery turned to him, red-faced, and nearly shouted, "When on the mat, I'm a wrestler, not a girl!"

"Okay, then," Kyle said, taking a step back. "Does that mean you're not quitting the team?"

"No, I'm not," Avery said, already walking away from him. "I thought about it, but my brothers would never let me hear the end of it if I did. They expect me to have a trophy next to theirs one day."

"Well, good," Kyle said. "See you at practice."

* * *

Kyle was happy to have Avery back at practice that afternoon, but Spider was still hardly talking to him, and Brandon and Ryan were still shooting him dirty looks across the room.

I hope Avery challenges one of them and wins. That'll show them, Kyle thought. But Avery didn't challenge anyone that day.

Kyle, however, decided to challenge Kenny again, even though he didn't expect to win. *If nothing else, it'll be good training,* he thought.

His second wrestle-off with Kenny didn't go much better than the first. Not only was Kenny strong and fast, he also had his moves down. At one point, he even darted under Kyle and took him down with a fireman's carry, lifting Kyle up over his shoulders and then throwing him to the mat.

Kyle was stunned for a moment, and Kenny almost scored a near fall on him. Luckily Kyle was able to roll onto his stomach before his shoulders hit the mat.

Losing the wrestle-off to Kenny meant Kyle would stay on B squad. But he wasn't far from weighing in at 175. *And once I make that weight, I have a good shot at getting back on the A squad,* he thought.

* * *

At the meet on Friday, Kyle sat next to Avery again. He was amazed at how focused she was on all the matches — especially Brandon's, Ryan's, and Spider's. It was like she was countering every move they made in her mind.

She's a wrestler, no doubt, Kyle thought.

Brandon lost a tough match at the 106 slot, but both Ryan and Spider won theirs, so the meet was off to a good start for the Jets.

"So, which one of them are you going to challenge on Monday?" Kyle asked. He sort of meant it as a joke, but Avery answered seriously.

"Ryan," she said.

"Wait, are you serious? Why? Brandon lost," Kyle said. "Or are you hoping to get revenge on Ryan for what he said the other day?"

"Kind of," she said, smiling. "But also because the guy Brandon lost to won his weight class at the citywide invite last year. And Brandon is one of our best wrestlers. That was a tough match. Plus, I'd have to drop a few pounds to challenge at 106."

Kyle nodded. Avery had clearly given this a lot of thought.

When it was time for the 175 match, Kyle started paying closer attention. Their A-squad wrestler at the 175 weight, Liam, was in eighth grade. He was big and strong. He liked to go on the attack and just pound his opponents. He had an inch or two on Kyle, but Kyle was quicker.

"Try a duck under," Avery said out of the blue.

"What?" Kyle replied.

"When you challenge Liam on Monday, try a duck under," she explained. "He leans forward too much when he goes to grapple. Plus, he's taller than you. He'd fall for a quick duck under."

"Thanks," Kyle said.

Then Avery yelled, "Come on, Liam!" Just because they were talking about how Kyle could beat Liam at a wrestle-off didn't mean that they wanted him to lose his match.

Unfortunately, Liam did end up losing. But by then, the Jets were so far ahead it didn't matter. And when Kenny won his match to close out the tournament, Kyle was so happy for his team that he wasn't even bothered by the fact that he was no longer the heavyweight.

CHAPTER 9

MAKING WEIGHT

Next Monday afternoon, just before practice, Kyle strolled by Avery's locker.

"Hey, Tank. What's up?" Avery said as Kyle walked by.

"I'm doing it today," Kyle said. He knew she'd understand what he meant — that today was the day he'd challenge Liam for the A-squad 175 spot.

"Really?" she said. "Good luck."

"Thanks," Kyle replied. "See you at practice."

Hopefully I won't need luck, though, he thought.

Kyle had been practicing the guillotine at home as often as his dad would let him, and he'd spent some time over the weekend studying the duck under Avery had suggested he try on Liam.

Kyle rushed to get to Spider's locker next. He wanted to get there before his friend could dump his school things off and head to the locker room.

"What's up, Spider?" Kyle asked as his friend approached the locker.

"Not much," was all Spider said.

"You know, Avery wasn't gunning for your spot," Kyle said.

Spider perked up and tilted his head to listen.

"She only wanted to wrestle at 120 because you wanted to wrestle at 126," Kyle explained.

"Really?" Spider asked, not totally convinced.

"Really," Kyle replied.

"So she's not going to challenge me to a wrestle-off?" Spider asked. "Everyone would tease me if a girl beat me."

I knew it, Kyle thought. "She's not a girl on the mat," he said, borrowing Avery's line. "She's a wrestler. You'd be losing to a talented, Spangle-trained wrestler."

"Yeah, I guess you're right," Spider admitted. He grabbed his things out of his locker, and the two of them headed to the wrestling room.

"So I did it," Kyle said as they walked.

"Did what?" Spider asked, confused.

"Cut down to 175," Kyle replied. "I was 176 when I weighed myself at home, but I think can hit 175 by Friday."

"Aw, man, Liam's going to be so bummed," Spider said.

"Hey, it's for the good of the team," Kyle said.

"True," Spider replied.

Kyle and his best friend walked into the wrestling room and sat down. When Coach asked if there were any challenges, Kyle stood up said, "Going for 175, A squad."

The whole team was surprised that Kyle would wrestle as anything but a heavyweight.

Coach raised an eyebrow. "You sure you can make that weight?" he asked.

"I weighed 176 earlier today," Kyle replied.

That news made Coach smile. "Good to hear," he said. "Anyone else challenging today?"

"I am," Avery said. "A squad, 113." She stood and motioned to Ryan, who looked mad about it.

Coach let Avery and Ryan wrestle first. Kyle was nervous for Avery as she walked out to the mat. Ryan had strength and size on her. But Avery had skill and determination.

Kyle watched and silently cheered Avery on from the sidelines as she went for a double-leg takedown, darting down to wrap up both of Ryan's legs. He shoved her to the mat and tried to tie her up, staying on top of her to keep her from escaping. Coach wasn't happy about that and penalized Ryan a point for stalling.

Once they were back up off the mat, Avery went for a leg sweep, using her front foot to knock Ryan's legs out from under him, tripping him up and scoring the takedown. But before she could get him on his back, he spun out for an escape.

Ryan might have a size advantage, but Avery is fast and has better moves, Kyle thought as he looked on. *They're pretty evenly matched.*

Coach eventually called the match a tie. Both wrestlers got up red-faced and breathing hard. Kyle hadn't realized just how good Avery was. It seemed that no one on the team had, until now.

Coach began clapping, and everyone else followed suit. "Well wrestled, you two," he said. "Ryan will keep his spot on A squad . . . for now."

Surprisingly, Avery didn't look upset about that. She was all smiles after receiving a round of applause from her teammates.

Then it was time for Kyle's wrestle-off with Liam. When Coach blew the whistle, Liam didn't waste any time attacking. Kyle was ready for him, though. When Liam charged, lumbering forward, Kyle brushed his right hand aside and ducked down under his shoulder as Liam rushed past. Kyle wrapped his arms around Liam's waist, lifting him off the ground and taking him to the mat. That was two points for a duck-under takedown.

Before Liam could recover from being slammed down on the mat, Kyle wrapped him up in a cradle with one arm around his neck and the other around a leg. Then Kyle rolled Liam onto his back, locking him in a guillotine.

Kyle kept control, and the match didn't last much longer. After a particularly hard-fought round, Kyle heard Coach's whistle and then, "Match goes to Kyle!"

Kyle was thrilled as he watched Coach change the rankings on the whiteboard. He was back on A squad. Both Spider and Avery walked over and high-fived him.

"You were awesome!" Spider nearly shouted.

"That duck under worked," Avery said.

There was an awkward silence as Kyle's old friend and his new one both stared down at their feet, not knowing what to say to one another. Avery finally broke the silence. "Hey, Spider."

"Hey," he said, blushing.

That's probably one of the only words Spider has said to a girl all year, Kyle thought.

Kyle turned to Avery. "I owe you, Avery," he said. Then, turning toward Spider, Kyle explained, "Avery suggested I try that duck under on Liam."

"Really?" Spider said. His eyes lit up as he looked at Avery. And suddenly, it was like a wall had come down between them. Instead of seeing Avery as just another girl he was too nervous to talk to, Spider started talking to her like he'd talk to any wrestler. "That's some great advice."

Just then, Kenny came walking over to the three of them. "Hey," he said. Looking right at

Kyle, he added, "Good to have you back on A squad."

"Thanks, Kenny," Kyle said, surprised. It was the most he'd ever heard Kenny speak.

Then Avery piped up with an even bigger surprise. "Hey, do you guys wanna have dinner with me, Kenny, and my dad?" she asked Spider and Kyle. "He's taking us out to eat after practice."

Did I hear that right? Kyle thought. *Dinner with Coach Spangle?*

"Yeah!" Kyle and Spider responded in unison.

The thought of meeting Coach Spangle made Kyle nervous. His wrestling program had produced more state tournament winners than any other school. He was a living legend, and both Kyle and Spider hoped to wrestle for him in high school next year.

After quick calls to their parents, Spider and Kyle both got the okay to go out to dinner, and soon Avery's dad was there to pick them all up in his car. Kenny sat quietly up front with his uncle while Avery, Kyle, and Spider sat in back.

When they got to the restaurant, Coach Spangle ordered the turkey breast with grilled veggies. The young wrestlers all did the same.

"I like to eat like my wrestlers — healthy," Avery's dad said after everyone had ordered.

"Yeah, but you should see him eat ice cream during the off-season," Avery teased.

"We call him Two Scoops," Kenny quipped.

Spider and Kyle were surprised by Kenny's joke, since he hardly ever talked during practice.

For most of dinner, the wrestlers sat back and listened as Avery's dad told stories. He recalled matches he'd been in during his wrestling days. He talked about some of the best wrestlers he'd coached over the years at Ben Franklin.

After a while, Coach Spangle turned the conversation to Spider. "Avery says you've been trying to move up a weight class," he said.

Spider looked down at his food, stirring it with his fork. "Yeah," he replied, embarrassed.

"Some people think heavyweights get all the glory," Coach Spangle said. "But all the matches count for the same amount of points. You should wrestle at the weight that feels natural to you."

Kyle saw Spider's face light up. Kyle had tried to tell him just that. But it was one thing getting advice from a friend and teammate and another hearing it from the top wrestling coach in the state.

Then Coach Spangle turned to Kyle. "And I hear you've been giving Kenny a run for his money at heavyweight," he said.

Kyle felt his face get hot. He was happy that Coach Spangle knew he'd been working hard.

"Yeah, you're one of the best wrestlers I've faced," Kenny said to Kyle. "Our team will dominate now that you're back on A squad."

Once the crew finished eating, Avery's dad drove Kyle and Spider home. Since the two friends lived around the corner from one another, they got out of the car together, thanking Coach Spangle for dinner and the ride.

"You know," Spider said after he slammed the car door shut, "Avery said her dad will be at the meet this week."

Kyle was surprised. Not about Coach Spangle being at the meet, which was exciting, but that Spider was talking to Avery . . . without Kyle there.

"I apologized for being mean to her that one day," Spider continued. "Just so you know."

"Thanks for doing that," Kyle said. "It was the right thing to do."

"Yeah," Spider agreed. "You were right about her. She's just a wrestler like the rest of us. Well, see you tomorrow." Then he turned away from Kyle and walked toward his house.

Kyle smiled. It felt like his team was coming back together at just the right time.

CHAPTER 10

A SQUAD

Sure enough, Coach Spangle was at the meet against Emerson on Friday. As if that wasn't cool enough, he even sat with the team, right next to Avery. As Kyle walked over to the bench, he sighed in relief. He'd just had his official weigh-in, and the scale showed he was just under 175 — perfect.

Kyle took a seat on the other side of Avery, opposite Coach Spangle. *If Avery's wrestle-off against Ryan earlier in the week didn't earn her some respect,* he thought, *having her dad show up here and sit with us on the bench sure will.*

"Did you make it?" Avery asked, referring to the weigh-in.

"Yep," Kyle said, smiling. "I came in at 175."

But now that the weigh-ins were complete, the pressure was on. All of the ninth graders, Kyle included, wanted to do well and show off for Coach Spangle. They knew if they impressed him, he might invite them to practice with the varsity team after the junior high season ended.

Things started off okay for the Jets. Brandon easily won his match with a major decision, scoring four team points at the A-squad 106 spot. Unfortunately, Ryan was up next at the 113 spot, and he lost his match.

Spider's match at 120 was tough. The kid he was up against was small, strong, and fast. He'd shot in for a double-leg takedown right away, wrapping both of Spider's legs and throwing him onto his back. Spider was able to escape, but he was slowly falling behind.

At the start of the second period, Spider was on the bottom in defensive position. When the referee blew the whistle, Spider spun around for a quick sit out to get separation from his opponent.

Then he went for one of those moves that made Spider amazing to watch. He somersaulted for an escape, performed a granby by sidestepping, flipped over his opponent, and drove him to the mat. Before the other wrestler could recover, Spider had him in a cradle. With one arm around his opponent's neck and one arm around the back of his knee, Spider clasped his hands together, making it nearly impossible for the other wrestler to escape.

Next Spider scored a reversal by getting on top of his opponent, earning two points. He scored another two points for a near fall, almost pinning his opponent, but the other wrestler escaped before it was too late. That almost evened up the match. The score was now 10–11.

Spider's opponent must have been winded, because the next time he shot in for a takedown, he was a little too slow. Spider got him in a headlock, wrapping his arms around his opponent's neck. He eventually drove his opponent down to the mat for a takedown. Those two points put Spider in the lead, and he held on to win 14–12.

As Spider walked off the mat, his teammates gathered around him for high fives.

"Nice moves out there. Where'd you pick up that granby?" Kyle asked.

"It's something Avery taught me in practice the other day," Spider said with a smile.

Spider must be learning that there are advantages to being friends with the daughter of the best high school wrestling coach in the state, Kyle thought.

During the next few matches, Kyle tried to sit back and relax, but he was nervous. It was a close meet, and everybody's score mattered. Plus he had his own match to worry about. He wasn't exactly facing an easy opponent. Emerson's 175 wrestler was Brian Mitchel, a ninth grader who had won his weight class at last year's citywide invite.

As if that wasn't enough, Coach Spangle was there to watch Kyle's first real match at the 175 weight class. It was a tremendous opportunity to show Coach Spangle his strengths, but the pressure was on.

As Kyle's turn to wrestle slowly approached, the Jets were losing to Emerson by a few points. Kyle knew that Kenny would put up a good fight after him in the heavyweight match, but he also knew that if he lost this match badly, he could lose the entire meet for his team.

And what would Coach Spangle think then? Kyle thought as he nervously tapped his feet on the ground.

CHAPTER 11

AN INVITATION

When Kyle's match was announced, he walked out to the center mat and bumped fists with Brian. Then the referee blew his whistle to start the match. Brian was tall, lean, and quick. He immediately rushed in to tie up Kyle's hands, probably hoping to use his height as leverage to force Kyle to the mat. But Kyle had been going up against taller wrestlers all his life, so this tactic wasn't new.

Plus, I have a new trick of my own, Kyle reminded himself. Kyle swatted Brian's right hand out of the way and ducked under his shoulder, wrapping his arms around his opponent's waist to try to get him off his feet. Brian fought harder against the duck under than Liam had, but eventually, Kyle got him to the mat for a takedown, earning two points. Brian quickly recovered and spun out of Kyle's grasp, earning an escape for one point. Kyle was up 2–1.

The same series of moves kept repeating itself throughout the match. One of the wrestlers would get the takedown and then the other would spin out for an escape. The two were evenly matched.

At the start of the third period, the score was tied at nine. Kyle had the top position, and Brian got down on his hands and knees in defensive starting position. Kyle leaned over him, left hand on Brian's left arm, right hand on his stomach.

Now it's time to bust out the guillotine, Kyle thought. *But I have to be quick. I bet Brian will go for the sit out in hopes of scoring an escape.*

The referee blew the whistle. As Brian went to escape, Kyle wrapped his right leg around Brian's. He hooked Brian's left arm with his right, then ducked down, somersaulting over his opponent. They both rolled over, and Brian ended up on his back. Kyle held him there for the count of two, scoring a near fall.

That move must have angered Brian. He threw an elbow at Kyle's jaw to try to break out of the hold.

The ref called the move unnecessary roughness, which gave Kyle an extra point. Plus it meant they would start back in referee position, which meant Kyle would be on top.

When they started wrestling again, Brian managed to escape from the bottom position, scoring a point for an escape. Then he charged at Kyle.

Kyle was ready with a move he had seen both Avery and Kenny use often — an arm drag with a single-leg takedown. By tugging on Brian's arm, Kyle got him off balance. Then he shot in, grabbing his opponent's leg and lifting it into the air.

Brian went down on his back, and Kyle scored two points for the takedown. He now had a good lead, so after that, he just fought to keep Brian down on the mat to prevent him from scoring any more points.

By the time Brian was able to escape and earn a point, it was too late. Match over!

Spider met Kyle with a high five as he walked off the mat. "The Tank is back!" he shouted.

* * *

The team was excited at they got on the bus to head back to school. With Kyle's winning decision for three team points, and Kenny's major decision for four, the Jets had walked away with the victory.

On the way home, Kyle and Spider sat beside one another at the back of the bus near Kenny and the other A-squad wrestlers.

As happy as the team was about the win, there was still one more surprise in store for them before the end of the night.

Instead of sitting up front with Coach Branberg, Coach Spangle came to join them at the back of the bus. Looking around at the group, he said, "There are a few wrestlers I'd like to invite to join the varsity team for practice after winter break. Kyle, Spider, Trevor — would you like to practice with my team in a couple weeks?"

There was some cheering from the other wrestlers as they congratulated their teammates.

Kyle and Spider sat still for a moment, unable to believe it. Then they looked at one another, their eyes wide, and shouted, "Yeah!" as they high-fived.

This is turning out to be my year after all, Kyle thought, grinning from ear to ear.

ABOUT THE AUTHOR

Blake Hoena grew up in central Wisconsin, where he wrote stories about robots conquering the moon and trolls lumbering around the woods behind his parents' house. He now lives in St. Paul, Minnesota, with his wife, two kids, a dog, and a couple of cats. Blake continues to make up stories about things like space aliens and superheroes, and he has written more than seventy chapter books and graphic novels for children.

GLOSSARY

confidence (KAHN-fi-duhns)—a strong belief in one's own abilities

disinfectant (diss-in-FEK-tuhnt)—a chemical used to kill germs

forfeit (FOR-fit)—to give up

grapple (GRAP-uhl)—to be in a close physical struggle with someone

invitational (in-vuh-TAY-shuh-nuhl)—a competition open only to those who are invited

maximum (MAK-suh-muhm)—the largest amount possible

penalize (PEE-nuh-lize)—to punish someone or to put someone at a disadvantage

singlet (SING-let)—a shirt or uniform that has no sleeves or collar and is used for playing sports

stance (STANTS)—the position of the body

tactic (TAK-tik)—a plan or method to achieve a goal

DISCUSSION QUESTIONS

1. Spider gets upset with Kyle when he befriends Avery, the only girl on the wrestling team. Why do you think Spider was so angry? Talk about some possible reasons.

2. Kyle decides to lose weight so he can get back on the A squad. Do you think he made the right choice? Or should he have stayed at the heavyweight position and tried to beat Kenny? Talk about your opinion.

3. Have you ever felt disappointed like Kyle did when he was moved down to the B squad? Talk about what you did to make yourself feel better.

WRITING PROMPTS

1. When Kyle decides to lose weight, he knows he needs to be healthy about it. Imagine you're Kyle and write out a weeklong healthy meal plan, including snacks!

2. At first, Kyle doesn't want to give up on wrestling as a heavyweight, but eventually, Avery convinces him it would be best for the team. Write about a time when you did something for the benefit of a group.

3. Imagine you are Kyle. Write a letter to Spider asking him why he has been distant. What do you want to say to him?

MATCH SCORING

During a match, wrestlers receive points for different moves they perform. The wrestler with the most match points at the end wins. Here's how those points are won:

ESCAPE (1 POINT)—when down on the mat, a wrestler breaks an opponent's hold and gets back to his or her feet

STALLING (1 POINT)—if a wrestler purposely halts the action during a match, a point goes to the opponent

ILLEGAL HOLD, UNSPORTSMANLIKE CONDUCT, OR UNNECESSARY ROUGHNESS (1 POINT)—when a wrestler performs a hold or move excessively hard, a referee can call it illegal, and a point goes to the opponent

TAKEDOWN (2 POINTS)—when a wrestler takes an opponent down to the mat and has control

REVERSAL (2 POINTS)—a wrestler breaks an opponent's hold and gains control, staying down on the mat

NEAR FALL (2 POINTS)—when a wrestler almost gets a pin and holds an opponent there for two seconds; the wrestler earns three points for holding the opponent for five seconds

MEET SCORING

Wrestlers score team points for winning their matches. The team with the most team points at the end of a meet wins. Here is how these points are given out:

DECISION (3 TEAM POINTS)—for winning a match by less than eight match points

MAJOR DECISION (4 TEAM POINTS)—for winning a match by eight to fourteen match points

TECHNICAL FALL (5 TEAM POINTS)—for having a fifteen-match-point lead on an opponent

PIN (6 TEAM POINTS)—for winning a match by pinning an opponent

FORFEIT, DEFAULT, OR DISQUALIFICATION (6 TEAM POINTS)—winning a match because an opponent chooses not to or is unable to wrestle